Fertile for the Mafia Billionaire

Willow Watkins

Copyright Page

Contents

Chapter One

♥

Rosalie

I can't breathe in this dress.

Not just because the corset is too tight. It feels like it's crushing my ribs, squeezing the air right out of my lungs. But it's more than that. It's the weight of everything pressing down on me at once. The satin, the lace, the veil, the expectations.

I sit stiffly in the back seat of the car, my hands folded tight in my lap. The window beside me is foggy, even though the air conditioning is on full blast. Or maybe it's just me. My palms are sweating, my stomach is in knots, and my heart is doing this fluttery, panicked thing that makes me want to crawl out of my skin.

My father is beside me, staring straight ahead like he's already checked out. Like this whole thing doesn't even matter to him anymore.

Maybe it never did.

The silence in the car is thick and uncomfortable. It's always like this with him lately. Tense. Cold. And no matter how many times I try to talk to him, to reach him, it's like I don't exist unless I'm agreeing with him.

But I try again. I have to.

"Please, Daddy," I whisper, my voice barely steady. "I can't do this. I don't love him."

He doesn't even blink. Doesn't turn to look at me.

"This isn't about love, Rosalie." His voice is calm. Detached. Like he's explaining something obvious to a child. "It's about loyalty. You're doing your duty."

My throat tightens. I turn my body towards him, just a little, fingers clutching the soft fabric of my dress. "But I barely know him. And the parts of him I do know, I don't like. He's... he's not kind. He's cold. I don't want to..."

He cuts me off with a sharp look. Finally, he sees me. But I almost wish he didn't. His eyes are hard. Unforgiving.

"Gregory Delacroix is the future of my company," he says, his voice sharp as a blade. "He's already bought out our debt, and with this marriage, he's promised to invest five million more. In exchange for you."

My mouth goes dry.

"You're the price I have to pay for my company to succeed," he adds, like it's nothing. "And I'm more than happy to pay it."

I feel like I'm going to be sick.

He turns back to the front, unbothered, straightening the cuffs of his tuxedo like we are just casually discussing the weather.

I don't speak. I can't. I'm too busy fighting back the tears and the bile threatening to rise up in my throat. My father has always been controlling. But it still hurts to hear that he sees me as nothing more than a pawn to be used to ensure the future of his company.

"You should feel honored," he says after a few moments of silence. "A man like that could have anybody, and he's willing to pay five million for you."

My heart is pounding. Every word he says just confirms what I already knew. Gregory isn't marrying me because he loves me. He's marrying me to own me. Just like he wants to own my father's empire.

He's not warm or charming. He's the kind of man who talks over me and corrects me. He doesn't smile at me. He assesses me, like I'm an acquisition.

Like I'm something to consume.

And my father sees nothing wrong with that.

"I gave you life," he says, his voice low and tight. "And it's my right to hand you over to someone else if I see fit."

I freeze, my breath catching in my throat.

He looks away again like he didn't just say something that shattered me into a hundred tiny pieces.

Outside the window, the buildings are blurring past. We're getting close now.

My hands are shaking in my lap. I fold them tighter, trying to make them stop. But I can't stop the ache in my chest, or the cold sinking into my bones. It feels like my body is warning me not to go through with this.

Don't walk into the church. Don't become his.

But the car keeps moving. And my father sits beside me like nothing is wrong. Like selling his daughter off is just another business deal that needs to be made.

Then the car slows, and through the tinted glass, I catch a glimpse of the front of the church.

Cameras flash in bursts like fireworks. Security in dark suits line the steps. Curious onlookers cluster just beyond the barricades, craning their necks for a better view. There's even a handful of reporters shouting questions to no one in particular, all of them waiting to catch a glimpse of the blushing bride - me.

My face might be hidden, but it doesn't stop the press from snapping photos.

The Wedding of the Year. That's what they've been calling it. A high-society merger. A fairytale romance. Except there's no prince, no magic, and no choice. Just a contract. A transaction dressed up in white silk and floral arrangements.

I grip the edge of the seat as the church steps fall away behind us.

The car doesn't stop.

Instead, we glide past the crowd, down a quiet side road. Around the corner and out of sight. The noise fades, replaced by the soft hum of the engine and the beat of my own heart pounding in my ears.

We pull up to a heavy iron gate tucked behind a row of hedges. It creaks open slowly, revealing a narrow driveway that leads behind the church.

The back entrance. Hidden. Out of view of the crowds.

"They don't need to see you until after the deal is done," my father mutters while glancing down at his phone.

That line hits harder than anything he's said. He could have said after the vows. Or after the ceremony.

But he chose to say after the deal.

Like I'm just a product and my unveiling is nothing more than a formality after the ink is dry.

I press my lips together, trying not to cry. If I cry now, my makeup will smudge, and I know Gregory well enough to know he won't like that. He wants perfection. Silent, polished, obedient perfection.

I look down at my hands, at the soft pink manicure the stylist chose to match my bouquet. They don't feel like my hands. Nothing about today feels like it's mine.

The car slows to a stop in the shade of a stone wall, and there's a private door up ahead.

I don't know how long we sit there in silence. It might be seconds. Or it might be minutes. But every tick of the clock makes my skin crawl even more.

My father's phone buzzes. He glances at the screen, his expression sharpening.

"This is important," he mutters, opening the car door. "Stay here. I need to take this in private."

Then he's gone, stepping away with the phone pressed to his ear, his voice already low and brisk as he walks towards the far end of the courtyard.

And just like that, I'm alone.

Alone in the back of a car. Wearing a dress that cost more than I'll probably ever make in my life. Waiting to be walked down an aisle I don't want to walk.

For a moment, the silence wraps around me, and I begin to wonder... is this my last chance?

My fingers twist the edge of my veil, the delicate lace catching against the tips of my manicured nails. I'm not even aware I'm doing it until I hear the faint rip of thread. But I don't stop.

My heart is pounding too hard, my mind racing too fast. Every breath feels shallow, like I'm only pretending to breathe.

Maybe if I sit very still, if I don't move, time will stop. Maybe this whole day will unravel like the edge of this veil, thread by thread, until none of it is real anymore.

I stare out the window. The sky is too blue. The world too calm. Everything in me is screaming that this all feels wrong.

And then there's movement.

Out of the corner of my eye, I catch a flicker of motion. A door opens near the side of the church.

Gregory.

He steps halfway out, scanning the lot like he's checking on a delivery. His gaze lands on the car. Lands on me.

And then he smirks.

Nothing about it is warm. It's not even polite. And it's certainly not the way a groom should be looking at his bride on their wedding day.

It's the smirk of a man who thinks he's already won. Like I'm a signature on a contract. A pretty little clause he negotiated and now gets to own.

There's no affection in his eyes. No nervous excitement. No joy.

Just calculation. Possession. Victory.

He turns and disappears back into the building without a second glance.

That look is all I need. I can't do this. I won't marry him. And I don't give a damn what my father or Gregory have to say about it.

I can't breathe. My chest is rising too fast. My hands are shaking. But I don't let myself hesitate. There isn't time for that. So I take one deep breath. Then another.

I kick off my shoes. The heels tumble to the floor of the car with a soft thud, like the sound of something precious being discarded.

But I don't feel precious. I feel like prey captured in the claws of two animals who couldn't care less about me.

My hand hovers over the door handle. My pulse is hammering in my throat, my ears, my fingertips. I press down, slowly and carefully, until the door clicks open just enough.

I peek out. My father isn't looking this way. He's still on his call, pacing, gesturing sharply with his free hand.

This is it. My one and only chance before I'm given away to somebody I hate.

I slip out, holding the edge of my gown up with both hands.

"Miss?" the driver calls out behind me, his voice tight with confusion. "Miss, wait... you can't..."

But I'm already running.

"Stop! You can't just... hey!"

I hear his door slam. The scuff of his shoes. The wheeze of effort as he tries to catch up to me. But he's not that fast. Maybe he would have been if he were two decades younger and at least a hundred pounds lighter. Not anymore, though.

My veil tears loose, whipped away by the wind. I let it go. My bare feet slap against the pavement. The ground is hot and rough, and my soles are already hurting.

But I don't care. I keep running.

My lungs burn. My dress is snagged and filthy. There's a rip in the hem now as it drags along behind me like a battle flag. My breath scrapes in and out of me like I've swallowed fire.

I don't know how far I've run. But I don't stop. Not yet. I can't.

I turn a corner... then another.

The pavement changes beneath my feet. It's smoother now. Colder. The noise of the church has faded completely behind me, swallowed by the tighter streets and higher walls.

There's a narrow alley ahead, tucked between two aging buildings, shadowed and empty. I slip into it, pressing my back to the cool stone.

And finally, I stop.

My hand covers my mouth, trying to catch the sob that wants to break free. Not because I'm sad. But because I made it.

Because I did it.

Because for the first time in my life, I didn't ask permission. I didn't wait for someone else to tell me who to be, or where to go, or what to want.

I chose this for myself.

Terror coils tight in my belly, but it's laced with something else. Something hot and electric. Something that feels a lot like hope.

Maybe I'm lost. Maybe I've just destroyed everything. Maybe I've walked away from the only protection I've ever known.

But for the first time in my life, I don't feel like a bird in a cage. I feel like a woman who just broke the damn lock.

I might not know where I'm going from here. But whatever comes next, it'll be mine. My mistake. My miracle. My choice.

Chapter Two

♥

Matteo

The sea is calm today. The kind of calm that unnerves men like me.

It stretches out the front of my villa, soft waves kissing the rocks below like it has nowhere better to be. Blue skies. Light breeze. No blood in the water. No screams on the wind. It should feel like peace.

But it doesn't.

I lean against the stone railing of the balcony. From up here, the world looks almost manageable. Distant. Tame. It's a lie, of course. But I let myself pretend.

This place, my villa, is meant to be a retreat. A quiet corner of the coast that the outside world forgets exists. When the wolves start snapping at each other's throats back in the city, I come here. I let my men handle the noise while I wait to see who bleeds first.

But I'm not built for stillness.

I haven't slept more than four hours in two days. Not because I'm worried. No one in my world would dare come for me directly. They know better. I'm the name that's whispered in the darkness, the shadow that makes lesser men fall in line. Matteo De Rossi isn't someone you test unless you've already decided to die.

And yet, I feel... restless. There's a weight in my chest. Not anxiety. Not fear. Something else. An itch I can't scratch. Like I'm waiting for something I don't know I'm missing.

Maybe I just need coffee. Or to spill some blood. Either way, sitting here like some bored aristocrat isn't going to solve a damn thing.

I head back inside, grab my keys, and leave the villa behind. The town is only a few minutes down the cliff road. It's small. Quiet. The kind of place no one expects to find a man like me.

The drive into town is short. Ten minutes if I take my time, five if I don't. I take my time.

Narrow roads wind along the cliff. The kind tourists think are charming and locals know will kill you if you blink at the wrong moment. I navigate them by instinct. I've been coming here for years. I own half of this damn coastline. But I rarely step foot in the town.

Today, something pulls me in that direction.

The car rumbles to a stop near the square. Cobblestone streets. Whitewashed buildings with blue shutters. It smells like salt and sun and espresso. I step out and let the air hit me, and I take a deep breath. It doesn't help the restless feeling, though.

I walk. No one stops me. No one stares too long. The people here know how to mind their own business, and the ones who don't usually learn after one quiet conversation with one of my men. It's peaceful. Quaint.

And then... I see her.

She's sitting in the front window of a cafe I've passed a few times but never entered. It's a small place with wrought-iron chairs and tables that are too close together. Half the paint has peeled off the door. But she's inside like she was dropped there from another world.

She's leaning slightly forward, a chipped mug cradled between both hands like it's the only warmth she's got. Her clothes don't fit - cheap jeans and a cheap sweater, with the sleeves swallowing her fingers - but her posture is still regal. Straight spine. Neck long. She's got a dancer's grace, even in hiding.

And she is hiding. That much is obvious.

Her eyes keep flicking towards the door. The window. The street. She's not looking for someone. She's watching for danger. Every movement is quiet, careful. Like she could flee at any moment.

She's a runaway. Young, frightened, and alone.

And mine.

The word slams into me like a truck. It makes no sense. I've never seen her before. I don't know her name, her story, whether she's trouble herself or just running from it. But my body responds like it's already decided. Something deep and territorial curls in my chest, low and savage.

She belongs to me.

I don't move. Don't breathe. I just stare through the glass, drinking her in like a man dying of thirst. Something in her makes her look up, like there's some invisible tether tugging her gaze towards mine. Her eyes are big and brown. Haunted.

For a split second, she looks like she might run. But instead, she looks away, and I decide it's time to introduce myself to my woman. Even if she doesn't know that's what she is yet.

I push open the door to the cafe, and the bell overhead gives a tired, metallic jingle.

She looks up like she's been struck. Her eyes find mine instantly, wide and startled, like prey scenting danger. But she doesn't move. Doesn't run. She just watches.

And I watch her back.

There's a beat, just long enough to feel it in my chest, where we hold each other's gazes. It only lasts a moment, though, before she glances away again, tucking her chin down while her fingers tighten around the mug in her hands.

The barista mumbles something to me, and I order a black coffee without taking my eyes off the woman. My voice fills the small space. Calm. Controlled. People always listen to me when I speak. I rarely ever have to raise my voice.

I take the cup in hand and move towards her table, slowly, like I'm approaching a startled animal.

She notices, even though she doesn't look directly at me. Her shoulders rise ever so slightly, a defensive tension wrapping around her spine. But her eyes lift to mine again as I stop beside her table. She doesn't speak, though.

I gesture to the empty chair. "May I?"

There's a pause, and her lips part like she might say no. Then she nods once, slow and hesitant.

So I take the seat opposite hers, and suddenly, the restless feeling that has been bothering me for days disappears.

She's even more beautiful up close.

Not in the way the world usually defines it, though she'd pass that test with ease. No, it's something deeper. Something quieter. She has a softness that doesn't belong in this world. Big eyes framed by thick, dark lashes, wide and alert like a startled deer. There's a faint shadow beneath them, like she hasn't slept in days. Her lips, which are full, unpainted, and slightly chapped, are pressed together too tightly, as if she's holding something back. A secret. Or maybe a scream.

Her skin is as pale as porcelain, with the faintest flush of pink on her cheeks. And her hair is pulled back, but loose strands have slipped free to frame her face.

But it's not just how she looks. It's how she sits. Perfectly straight, with her spine rigid and her shoulders tight. Like she's holding herself in. Like she's afraid to take up space, to breathe too loudly.

It makes something dark twist low in my chest.

I want to see her loosen. Unfurl. I want her to know what it's like to take up room without apology. To feel safe enough to stretch her arms out wide and breathe.

My hands curl slightly underneath the table. It's involuntary. Primal. I'm too close to her and not close enough. My body reacts before my brain can catch up, with my heart beating harder and a heat pulsing low in my gut.

I've seen beauty before. I've used it and walked away from it without a second glance. But this isn't just beauty. It's something sacred and holy. And for the first time ever, I can imagine spending the rest of my life with someone.

She doesn't speak first. Instead, she just continues to watch me in between occasional glances towards the window.

"Are you from around here?" I ask, trying to keep my voice casual even though I feel anything but.

There's a flicker of hesitation before she offers a quiet, practiced response. "I'm just passing through."

I nod slowly, sipping my coffee. "I'm not staying long either. Just needed some peace and quiet."

Her brow furrows, like she can't figure me out. Good. A sweet, young thing like her shouldn't be able to.

"So you don't live here?" she asks.

I shrug. "I have a place here. Up along the cliffs. It's where I go for a few days whenever I need to get away from the real world, you know? But my main home is in the city."

She chuckles. "Must be nice to have two homes."

I tilt my head. Something about the way she says that makes me feel like she doesn't have anywhere she considers home. She returns my gaze, studying me like she's trying to decide if I'm dangerous.

I am... but not to her.

"Do you want to tell me your name?" I ask, my voice as soft as velvet.

There's another long silence before she finally gives a single shrug of her shoulders.

"Fair enough." I pause for a second, carefully considering my next words before speaking. "I don't know who hurt you, but they'll never get close again. I'll make sure of it."

That lands. I see the shift in her expression. The way her shoulders loosen, and she lets out a long breath. She still doesn't smile, but this is a start.

I lean forward, forearms braced on the table between us. "I won't ask where you come from. But do you at least know where you are going to?"

She draws her coffee cup closer, though it's long gone cold. Her fingers tremble around the chipped porcelain as if she needs something to hold on to. A tether. A shield.

"I don't have anywhere to go," she says so softly I almost miss it.

"Then you'll stay with me," I say, my voice soft but firm. "My villa isn't far. It's private. Safe. No one will bother you there. No one will find you."

Her eyes search mine, confused. Suspicious. A little spark of defiance flares beneath the fear.

"Why are you..." Her voice tightens. "What do you expect from me in return?"

There it is. Not just mistrust of me, but of the world. Of men. I don't flinch or take offense. She's not wrong to ask.

"Nothing," I say. "I don't want anything from you. I'm offering safety. No strings. No expectations. I just want you to be safe."

She studies me like she's waiting for the lie. But there isn't one, and she sees that.

The woman in front of me exhales, letting out a slow and shaky breath. Then she nods. "Okay."

She looks down at the table, then back up, her eyes a little clearer now. Still guarded, but softer.

"Rosalie," she says, her voice hesitant, as if she doesn't realize she's offering me the most precious gift. "My name is Rosalie."

Rosalie. It lands like a drug in my veins. Sweet. Dangerous. Addictive. And now that I've tasted her name, I already know I'll want the rest of her... forever.

Chapter Three

♥

Rosalie

When I wake up, for a second, I forget where I am.

The bed is too big. The sheets are soft. Everything smells clean, like lemons and salt water and something else I can't place. For a moment, I think maybe it was all a dream. That I just imagined the man at the cafe, and the way he watched me like he couldn't bear to look away.

But then I hear the ocean. Waves crashing somewhere beyond the window. And I remember it is all true. I'm in Matteo's villa.

I sit up slowly, rubbing my hands over my face. Judging by the bright sunlight shining through the window, I slept longer than I meant to.

The white walls of my temporary bedroom only make it seem even brighter, and the cream curtains move slightly as the breeze comes in through the open window. There's a big wardrobe in the corner, where all my new clothes hang. Clothes that had arrived at the villa less than an hour after I had. Clothes I hadn't asked for, but that Matteo knew I would need. Just like he somehow knew what size I needed.

He didn't even say anything about them. He just left them here for me to find. And I'm not used to people doing things without expecting something in return. Especially not men.

Before I came here, I sold my wedding dress to a pawnshop. I didn't get much for it, but it was enough for the second hand jeans and sweater I'd been wearing when I first met Matteo, and a bus ticket. I hitchhiked the rest of the way. The last guy who picked me up looked at my legs more than the road, so I made an excuse and got out. And that was how I'd ended up in this sleepy little town.

And then I'd seen him. Matteo.

He walked into that cafe like he owned the whole damn town. He was the epitome of tall, dark, and handsome, but there was something else about him, too. I could practically feel the danger rolling off him in waves, but that didn't stop my body from reacting to him.

My heart didn't just skip. It stumbled. And a slow, curling heat had started in the pit of my stomach before moving lower. All he'd done was walk into the cafe and I'd practically unraveled. And when he'd looked at me, the fear that had been chasing me for days since running away from my own wedding had just... disappeared.

I could hardly believe my luck when he had approached me and then offered me a place to stay. All with no strings attached, apparently.

I've always believed everything came with strings, but after three days of staying with him, he hasn't once asked me for anything in return for his kindness, and I'm not sure what to make of that.

I swing my legs out of bed and pad across the room barefoot. My toes sink into the thick rug, and I stop by the window to look out.

The sea is bright and blue and endless. The cliffs drop down into it like something out of a painting. And even though I know I should be planning where I'll run next, or what I'll do if Matteo turns out to be like all the other men in my life, I can't bring myself to move.

I just stand there, listening to the waves and letting myself feel safe, even if it's only for a minute.

With a sigh, I step away from the window and head towards the wardrobe. I run my fingers along all the clothes hanging up. There are jeans, a few long skirts, and simple cotton tops. Some sweaters that will fit a lot better than the second-hand one I bought myself. And a pretty dress. It's white, with tiny blue flowers on it. It looks like something you'd wear to a picnic.

I reach further back and pull out something else. It slips off the hanger like water between my hands. A silky, dusky blue nightdress with thin straps and lace at the hem. It's the kind of thing I'd never buy for myself. Far too sexy and revealing. But the idea that Matteo would have bought this for me has both confusion and arousal mingling in my stomach.

I try to shake it off. Try not to read too much into it. I hang the nightdress back up and move towards the bathroom, where toiletries line up on the counter. Shampoo. Conditioner. Toothbrush and toothpaste. A little tube of lip balm. Even tampons in the cupboard under the sink. He'd thought of everything I could need, and just left them here for me.

It all feels like too much kindness.

I brush my teeth and freshen up, deciding it's a nice enough day to wear the dress. By the time I make it outside, the sun is high in the sky, warming the stone under my bare feet. The terrace is quiet except for the waves, steady and slow below the cliff.

Matteo is there, sitting in one of the chairs with his legs stretched out in front of him and one arm slung over the back. His sunglasses are pushed on top of his head, and there's a phone in his hand. His eyes flick up when he sees me.

"Morning," he says.

His voice is deep and a little rough, like he hasn't spoken yet today. I don't know why that makes something shift in my stomach.

"Hi," I say, small and awkward.

There's a table between us, low and wide, set with foods like a hotel spread. A silver tray of cut fruit, with melon, berries and mango. Flaky pastries dusted in powdered sugar. A carafe of coffee and two mugs.

He nods towards the table. "Help yourself."

I hesitate. Then step closer and sit in the empty chair, tucking my feet up under me.

"Thanks," I murmur, as I pour myself a cup of coffee.

I steal glances at him when he's not looking. Which is harder than it should be, because somehow, he always seems to know when I do.

But right now, he's distracted. Reading something on his phone. His profile is sharp and still, with high cheekbones, a strong jaw, and that straight Roman nose. His mouth is full and unsmiling, but not unkind. Even when relaxed, there's something coiled beneath his skin. Like a patient wolf, stretched out and calm, but always watching.

He's wearing a plain white polo shirt and dark linen pants, loose and soft-looking but clearly expensive. His whole outfit whispers of understated luxury. And his body is big. So big. Broad chest and thick arms make the shirt cling to him in places, and my eyes linger where it stretches tight across his shoulders, tracing the slope of muscle beneath.

Just looking at him makes me feel breathless. An awareness of him pulses through me like heat under my skin. My heart races every time he looks at me. And when he speaks, his voice low and deep, my breath catches before I even know what he's said.

I don't understand why I feel this way around him. I shouldn't after everything I've been through. But despite the little voice in my head telling me to be wary, whenever he's close, I feel safe. Peaceful. And that makes him strangely addictive.

"Did you sleep okay?" he asks, finally breaking the silence.

I nod. "Yeah. I mean... yeah. Better than I have in a while."

His mouth lifts at the corners. Like he knows what that means without needing the details.

"Good," he says. "Hungry?"

I nod again, more shy this time.

He picks up a plate filled with almond covered pastries and holds it out to me. I tentatively reach out to take one, and my fingers brush against his.

It's barely even a touch, but it lights me up like he's touched every inch of me at once. A rush of warmth climbs my throat, floods my chest, and settles between my thighs.

I dip my head, hoping to hide the flush on my face, and take a bite of the pastry. If he notices how flustered I am by that simple touch, he doesn't say anything.

"Do you want to go for a walk later?" he asks instead. "There's a trail through the cliffs with a nice view."

I blink at him. "Yeah. Sure. That sounds nice."

He just nods and finishes his coffee while I eat the pastry and some fruit. Neither of us says anything, but the silence is not an awkward one.

I glance at him again, and my chest does that fluttery thing it does whenever he's near.

I'm not sure what game he's playing, or if it's even a game at all. But I think I might want to keep playing it for just a little while longer.

***

The wind tangles through my hair as we walk. The path curves along the cliffs and the ocean churns below us, deep and endless. It's beautiful here, with no one around for miles. I can't help wondering what it would be like to live somewhere like this, with the constant crash of the waves as my company.

I glance at Matteo from the corner of my eye. The wind presses his shirt to his chest, outlining hard muscle and broad shoulders. His hands are tucked into his pockets, and my mind drifts back to how our fingers had brushed this morning, and how that tiny touch had lit me up inside.

He doesn't speak until we reach a bend in the path, the sea opening wide before us. "Are you ready to tell me what you're running from yet? I might be able to help you."

His gaze lingers on the sea, as if he wants to give me privacy to decide what to say, even though we're standing side by side. He waits patiently as a battle wages inside of me. My brain is telling me not to trust him. Not to trust anybody. But my heart is telling me something different.

So far, he hasn't given me any reason to believe he wants to hurt me or use me. All he's done is take care of me and give me all the things I needed when I had nothing.

This seems like the least I could do for him.

"I left someone," I say quietly, my voice sounding small in the wind. "At the altar. He wasn't..." I pause and take a deep breath. "He wasn't kind, and he didn't love me. But my father was going to make me marry him anyway, because he wanted to sell me off like property just so he could get the money he needed to save his business."

Matteo goes very still beside me, but his eyes remain on the horizon, as if giving me space to speak.

"So I ran. It was spur of the moment. I saw a chance, and I took it. But I left behind everything and everybody..."

My throat tightens. I blink hard, but it's not enough to stop the tears that roll down my cheeks.

Matteo moves before I realize what is happening. One moment he's just beside me, the next his arms are around me, pulling me in close to his body.

I don't fight him.

His chest is solid against my cheek, and the faint scent of his cologne surrounds me, making me want to press closer. His heartbeat thuds steadily, a rhythmic drum against my ear, and his hand is warm on my back.

His presence is strong. Unwavering. Like a fortress.

And right now, that is exactly what I need.

So I let myself relax, and I wrap my arms around him, fingers clutching the fabric of his shirt. A heat coils low in my belly, curling through me with every second that I remain in his arms.

I tilt my head up, just slightly. His eyes meet mine, dark and stormy, and the look there... it steals the air from my lungs. There's hunger, yes. But something deeper, too. A kind of reverence I've never received before.

He leans in and I stop breathing. His own breath is hot against my lips, and I want to rise up on my toes. I want to kiss him. To feel his mouth against mine.

But before I can, he stops. Just a fraction away from my lips, so close and yet so far.

His voice is a low rumble. "Rosalie. I want to kiss you so damn badly. But not like this. Not when you're hurting. When I do it, I want it to be because it's what you really want. I don't want it to be a bad decision you made because you were feeling sad."

He pulls back, his thumb gently wiping away a stray tear from my cheek. I can't think of a thing to say.

Because he could have kissed me. Could have taken what he wanted, and I would have let him. But he waited.

He takes a step back, and I instantly miss his arms around me. But he takes my hand instead, linking his fingers with mine.

"Come on," he says, his voice softer than I've heard it before. "Let's head back."

And for the rest of the walk back, he doesn't let go.

Chapter Four

♥

Matteo

The clock ticks loud in the silence.

I'm sitting at the kitchen table, one hand wrapped around a glass of water I haven't touched, the other clenched around nothing. My jaw aches from the way I've been grinding it. I can't sleep. I can't stop thinking about her.

About what she told me on the cliffs.

Sold. Promised. Bartered like property by the one who should have protected her. Given away to another man for money and favors. And she was just... supposed to accept it.

I press my thumb hard into the bridge of my nose, trying to drain the tension behind my eyes. It doesn't help.

I want to find her father. Her ex-fiance. I want to bury them both so deep in the goddamn earth that nobody will ever find them.

But before I can do that, I need to find out as much as I can about my woman and her past. So I reach for my phone and call Luca. He's my right hand, my closest friend, and the only man I trust with something like this. Especially when it concerns Rosalie.

He answers on the second ring, his voice groggy. "Yeah?"

I don't bother with formalities. "Find me everything you can on a runaway bride named Rosalie. Early twenties. Was engaged to someone who had a lot of money, so he shouldn't be too hard to find. Look into it. I don't care how long it takes."

There's a beat of silence. Then a grunt. "Got it. I'll call when I have something."

I hang up and set the phone on the table. Stare at the shadows shifting across the tiled floor. I've made a career of hunting men like the ones she ran from. But this isn't just about a job.

This is personal.

She's in my house, and I won't let the past hurt her again. Not ever.

The soft sound of footsteps pulls my gaze towards the kitchen door. Rosalie stops when she sees me. Frozen. Wide-eyed. Like a doe caught in a beam of light. Her arms come up across her chest, folding in, like she wants to disappear. Or at least hide the delicious little nightdress that clings to every perfect curve of her body.

It's made of blue silk, held up by thin straps. And the way her perky nipples poke against the fabric, it's obvious she's not wearing much underneath it.

The sight of her in it hits me like a punch to the chest.

"I didn't think you'd be up," she says quickly, barely looking at me. Her voice is small, breathy. Embarrassed.

She tugs at the hem of the nightdress, like maybe it will magically grow longer. "I just found this in the wardrobe. I thought it was... pretty."

It is pretty. But Rosalie... she's something else.

"You're beautiful," I say, without hesitation.

Her eyes finally meet mine, and there's a storm of emotion swimming in them. Embarrassment. Confusion. Something warmer, too. Something like curiosity. Want.

I push my chair back slowly, the scrape of wood against the tile quiet in the thick night air. I tap my hand on my thigh, offering an invitation.

"Come here, Rosalie."

She hesitates for just a moment. Then she crosses the floor and lowers herself carefully into my lap.

My arms come around her instinctively. One on her lower back. The other curving around her thighs, anchoring her to me. She fits like she belongs in my lap.

And the silk of that nightdress? It's a fucking torture device. Smooth and delicate and clinging to skin that I've thought about every damn night since she walked into my world.

I don't let my hands roam, even though every cell in my body begs me to. I keep them respectful. Protective. Exactly where they need to be.

I'm so caught up in how it feels to have her close that it takes me a moment to realize she's not looking at me. Her lashes are lowered, her cheeks holding the slightest dusting of pink. And her lips are parted like she wants to say something but isn't sure how.

I drop my head, speaking low in her ear. "What's wrong, babygirl?"

The word does something to her. Her breath hitches, and I feel a shiver run down her spine. When she finally lifts her eyes to meet mine, they're wide and unsure, but burning with something deeper.

"I want..." She swallows. "I want you to kiss me, Matteo. I'm not sad anymore, but I still want it."

My heart kicks hard against my ribs, but I don't move. Not yet.

Rosalie takes a shaky breath, pushing the words out like they cost her something. "I've never... I've never been kissed. My father wouldn't allow it. Him and my fiance... they said I would be more valuable if I stayed untouched. So I'm sorry if I don't know what I'm doing."

The silence between us stretches tight, my jaw locked to keep from saying what I want to say. What I want to do to the men who made her believe her worth was something to be measured by her purity.

I breathe in slow. Deep. Centering myself.

Then I look her in the eye and say, "You're not valuable because you're untouched, Rosalie. You're valuable because of who you are. And I'm honestly glad that your ex-fiance didn't lay a finger on you, because he didn't deserve that honor. Because, babygirl, you deserve to only be touched by someone who worships you. Respects you. Loves you."

She whimpers softly, but I still don't move. I wait until she leans in first. It's just the smallest tilt of her chin, but it's enough.

I close the distance and press my mouth to hers, and her lips part tentatively. Soft. Sweet. And fuck, she tastes good.

I can't help it. My hands start moving. Up her spine, tracing over the silk, then down, following the dip in her waist and the flare of her hips. I groan at how perfect she feels beneath my hands, and she makes a little mewling noise that has my cock straining against the fabric of my pants.

And as much as I want to be gentle with her, those little sounds she makes have me wanting to just devour her.

So I slide one hand up to tangle in her hair, tilting her head to the perfect angle. And then I kiss her. Harder. Deeper. I slip my tongue between her lips, tasting her like she's a meal and I'm a starving man.

The kiss turns desperate. Hot. Messy. Her hips shift on my lap and her nightdress rises higher as her core presses up against the thick outline of my erection. I can feel the heat of her pussy even through my pants, and I grab her hip in my free hand, trying to pull her closer.

I tear my lips from hers just long enough to drag in a breath. "I want to put a baby in you, Rosalie."

The words rip out before I can stop them. Raw and possessive, and so fucking true.

She freezes, but I don't think she's scared. Her pupils are blown wide and her breath stutters. Another shift of her hips has her pressing more firmly against my hard cock, and the tiniest whimper slips from her red, swollen lips.

I dip my head, bringing my lips to her ear. "I want them to see that you're mine, babygirl. To see that they can never take you back. I want them to look at your belly and know you've got a man who can take care of you and who will never let anything happen to you."

"Matteo," she gasps, and my name on her lips makes my cock throb with a need to claim her virgin womb.

"Tell me you want it too, babygirl, and I'll make it happen. I'll take care of you. Worship you. Fill you with so much of my seed that you'll be pregnant by the end of the night."

Her hands slide up to my chest, and for a moment, I think she's going to push me away. But instead, her fingers tangle in my shirt.

"Yes," she whispers against my lips. "I want it, Matteo. I want you to be my first, and I want your baby inside me."

Those words almost fucking break me. Her voice is so soft and shy when she says them, but it detonates something feral in me. All the restraint I've fought to hold on to suddenly cracks.

Rosalie wants me. She wants me to fill her. To breed her.

My dick pulses hard beneath her, and I grip her hips with both hands, grounding myself with the feel of her curves, the silk gliding over her skin, the heat of her body under my fingers. My voice comes out low, guttural. Like it's been dragged from some place ancient and wild.

"Say it again, babygirl. Tell me what you want."

"I want…" Her breath hitches. "I want you to put a baby in me."

Fuck. That's it. That's all I can take.

I stand up with her in my arms like she weighs nothing. She squeals softly and wraps herself around me, clutching my shoulders as I carry her through the dark villa like she's already mine. Because she is.

"You're going to look so goddamn beautiful," I growl, pressing my lips to her temple as I head for my bedroom. "Round and full with my baby. Glowing with happiness because you know your man will always take good care of you and all our babies. No one else will ever touch you. No one else will ever get the chance."

She shivers against me, her breath coming faster. I can feel her heart racing where our chests press together.

I nudge the bedroom door open with my shoulder and lower her carefully to the bed as if she's sacred. Because, as far as I'm concerned, she is. I look down at her, taking in the rapid rise and fall of her chest, her flushed cheeks, and that little blue nightdress that clings to every soft curve.

And I wonder, what did I do to deserve such a perfect little angel in my life?

She sits up and reaches for the hem of her nightdress, pulling it over her head. Then she lies back on the sheets and looks up at me with a smile, so fucking trusting and innocent and willing.

My gaze roams slowly over her naked body while my cock strains painfully against my pants.

Her breasts are round and full, tipped with sweet, hard nipples that beg for my mouth. Her hips are full and lush, made to cushion the weight of a child. And her pussy… Jesus Christ. It's a pretty pink slit, the delicate lips glistening with her need.

I can't take it anymore.

I shrug off my shirt and pants, tossing them aside. And when I look down at Rosalie, she's staring at me, her eyes wide.

"Is something wrong, babygirl?"

"No," she whispers. "You're just... big."

The corner of my mouth lifts. "It'll fit, sweetheart. Don't worry. You're made for me."

And as much as I'd like to taste her, my need is too great. Too urgent.

So I climb onto the bed, caging her body beneath mine. She opens her legs, making room for me between them, and I trap my erection between our bodies, rolling my hips so the belly of my cock glides back and forth over her clit.

Rosalie lets out a gasp that would tempt the most devout man to sin, and her eyelids flutter. She wriggles beneath me, seeking the friction, and I press harder with my hips. Her wetness is coating my cock, letting me rub her slick clit easily, and her nipples brush against my chest with each movement.

"Please," she whispers. "Please stop teasing me, Matteo. I need you to make me yours."

"Oh, babygirl," I growl. "That's exactly what I'm going to do."

I slide one hand between us and grip the base of my cock, angling it towards her opening. Slowly, gently, I press the head inside her, and Rosalie's breath catches. Her walls clench, fighting the intrusion, but her nails dig into my biceps and her thighs spread wider, begging me to take her.

Her little virgin hole is so tight around the tip of my cock that I can barely move, and when I push another inch inside, she cries out.

"Does it hurt, babygirl?"

She shakes her head, her lashes damp. "No. It's... more than I expected. But please... don't stop. I need more."

I grit my teeth, fighting the urge to just slam inside her and rut until I've pumped her full of every drop of cum. The need to paint her insides with my seed, to really claim her, is overwhelming, and I have to keep reminding myself that this is her first time.

I have to be gentle.

My free hand trails down her side and I hook her leg around my hip, spreading her wider. Giving me better access.

With a low groan, I rock my hips, driving further into her. She whimpers, but there's a desperate edge to it. She arches her back, pressing her tits against my chest, and her head tips back.

I lean in and capture her throat with my mouth. Licking. Sucking. Nipping at the delicate flesh. And when I reach the curve of her shoulder, I bite down. Hard enough to mark her, but not enough to break the skin.

I need to mark her as mine.

"Yes," she cries, and her pussy flutters, clenching around my cock. "Oh God, Matteo. That feels... Oh. More. Please, more."

"So fucking sweet," I growl. "You're so fucking perfect, babygirl. I'm going to make sure the whole world knows you're mine."

I push in a little deeper, and her nails rake across my back. With a deep groan, I push again, and Rosalie's moan echoes through the room.

Her virginity is still resisting me, though, and her channel is so tight it's almost painful.

I reach between us and find her clit, rubbing the sensitive little bud with firm strokes. I work her until she's panting and moaning, her body bucking beneath me, and only then do I ease her thighs wider and drive in one final time.

She gasps as I bury myself deep inside her. Her eyes go wide, and her nails dig hard into my arms.

"Breathe, babygirl," I say. "Breathe."

And then, finally, her body relaxes.

I give her a second, my balls throbbing with the need to empty myself inside her. But then she lifts her hips, silently asking for more.

Slowly, I pull out and then slide back in. Rosalie gasps and then moans, her pussy pulsing.

"Oh... Oh. That's good. Matteo, please, keep doing that."

With a grin, I pull out and drive back in, starting a rhythm that has her gasping and moaning, her body rocking up to meet mine with each thrust. I can feel her tight channel relaxing around me ever so slightly, allowing me to glide deeper.

I can't wait to feel her come. To have her walls milk my cock.

"That's it, babygirl. You're doing so good. Now, give me everything, Rosalie. Show me what a good girl you are."

My thumb circles her clit faster, and she lets out a whimper. Then a moan.

"Please," she begs. "Please, Matteo. Keep going. I'm so close."

With a grin, I lean in and capture her lips, swallowing her cries as she tumbles over the edge. Her pussy squeezes my cock like a vise, and her whole body shudders beneath me.

"Good girl," I murmur, continuing to pump into her. "You're taking me so well, babygirl."

"Oh... Matteo," she breathes, her eyes glassy with bliss. "It's so much."

"But you're doing so good. Let me fill you up, babygirl. You're ready for it. Ready for my cum."

"Yes," she says. "Yes. Fill me, Matteo. Fill me."

"Look at me," I command, and she does.

Her eyes are hazy, and her lips are parted, and fuck, it's perfect.

My orgasm slams into me, and I roar as the hot rush of cum spurts from the head of my cock, coating Rosalie's channel with long jets of white. My hips continue to buck, fucking her hard and deep as I empty myself.

I kiss her roughly, possessively. Marking her all over again.

She's mine. Mine, and no one can ever take her away from me.

When I finally slow and stop, I roll to the side, bringing her with me so we're facing each other. I can't bear the thought of separating my body from hers, and I love the way she feels in my arms. Like she belongs there.

Her fingers trace patterns on my skin, and she lets out a contented sigh.

"Are you okay, babygirl?" I ask, brushing a strand of hair away from her cheek.

"Mmhmm," she mumbles, her eyes drifting closed. "More than okay."

I hold her tighter and press a kiss to her forehead. "Rest now, babygirl. I'll keep you safe while you sleep. Always."

And as her breathing grows slower, steadier, I make a vow to myself.

I will always protect her. Always love her.

She is mine, and no one will ever take her from me.

Chapter Five

♥

Rosalie

I wake up slowly. The kind of slow where it feels like I'm still dreaming. My body aches in places I didn't know could ache... but it's a good ache. The kind that makes me press my thighs together under the covers and smile to myself like I'm keeping a secret.

The room is quiet, the morning light soft and pale through the curtains. Matteo's bed smells like him. Clean, warm and masculine. I don't even remember falling asleep. Just the way he held me afterwards, the way he whispered in my ear.

His chest rises and falls as I rest my head on it, listening to the steady beat of his heart. I'm curled against him like I belong here, and his arm is wrapped tight around my waist. But it's his other hand I feel the most. It's buried in my hair, gripping gently but firmly, like even in his sleep he doesn't want to let me go.

I shift a little, trying not to wake him. But the second I move, his grip tightens. A deep sound hums in his throat.

"Where are you going, babygirl?" His voice is low and rough, still thick with sleep.

I freeze. "I didn't mean to wake you," I whisper. "I was just going to grab a shower and get cleaned up…"

"I'll come with you," he says.

My heart skips. "You don't have to if you want to sleep a little longer…"

"I want to." His hand brushes down my back, stopping just above my hip. "Let me take care of you. I'll go get the hot water running."

With that, he throws the covers off and climbs out of bed, and I take a moment to admire his bare ass as he walks towards the bathroom. When he disappears, I flop back against the pillow, a smile playing across my lips.

I can't believe I got this lucky.

Only a minute passes when I hear him calling my name, and when I enter the bathroom, he's already in the shower. I step in with him, and the heat instantly makes my muscles loosen up and my thoughts blur a little.

I stand still, watching the water bead on his skin, watching as the droplets run down the hard wall of muscle. But then he's reaching for a bottle of body wash.

"Turn around, babygirl," he says, his voice low and gentle.

I do as he says.

His hands are big and sure as they move over my back, slicking soap across my skin. He takes his time, like he's memorizing every part of me through touch. And even though he doesn't say much, I feel it in the way his fingers linger at my hips. In the way he presses a soft kiss to my shoulder before reaching for the shampoo.

"Close your eyes," he murmurs.

I tilt my head back. The water runs down my face as he lathers the shampoo into my hair with slow, careful movements. I've never had anyone do this for me before, and the way he touches me makes my chest ache.

He moves slowly and carefully, like he's handling something precious, and it makes something soft bloom in my chest. His big hands work the shampoo through my hair, and a quiet thought slips in before I can stop it. He's going to be a good father. It startles me a little, but it doesn't feel wrong. Not even close. My cheeks warm as I look down at my belly, wondering if he already put a baby there last night. God, I hope he did.

I know it's way too soon to have a baby with him, but my heart and body are unwilling to listen to reason. They know what they want, and it's him. And his babies. Preferably more than one.

Matteo turns me around, tilting my head back to rinse the shampoo out. Once the suds are gone, I open my eyes and see him staring down at me. There's so much intensity in his gaze, so much emotion.

For a moment, we just stand there. Close. Naked. His hands rest at my waist, thumbs stroking gently at my skin.

That's when I see them again. The scars. I'd seen them last night, but I had been so caught up in giving him my first time that it hadn't seemed like the right time to mention them. They stand out faintly beneath the water. I'm not exactly an expert, but I see at least two that look like they might have come from gunshot wounds. Another one looks like someone sliced a knife across his skin.

My heart clenches at the sight of them, and I raise my hand before I can stop myself, running my fingertips across the longest one.

"You got in a fight?" I ask softly, suspecting that doesn't come close to explaining the scars.

His eyes stay on mine, but his expression doesn't change. "I've had my share."

"Did it hurt?"

He hesitates for just a second. "A little."

I'm not stupid. To have this many scars, I know he'd had to have been involved in some seriously dangerous situations. And yet, I'm not scared. If anything, the scars make him seem more human. They remind me that he's real, not just a perfect god made of marble and strength and steel.

I swallow. "I think that maybe you have a lot of enemies."

He leans in close until our foreheads touch. "Yes, I do. But none of them are a threat to me. Or to my woman. Understand?"

My breath catches and my heart thuds. I nod.

He brushes a damp curl from my cheek, eyes locked on mine. "Good. Because no one touches what's mine, Rosalie. No one."

My legs feel shaky, but not from fear. From the way he looks at me like he'd burn down the whole world to keep me safe. There may be a dark part of his life that I don't know about yet. But I know who he is in his heart. In his soul. And that's more than enough for me.

Unable to resist, I let my hand slide down his chest, inching closer to the hard rod of flesh poking against my stomach. A little grunt slips out of his throat as my fingers wrap around his erection.

"Is this because of me?" I whisper.

"Yeah, babygirl. This is because of you." He groans and his hands drop to my ass, pulling me closer. "Tell me what you want, Rosalie."

"This." I give him a squeeze, and his hips jerk forward. "Inside me. Filling me with more of your seed."

His dark eyes flash with something feral. "You haven't changed your mind? You still want me to knock you up, babygirl?"

Heat blooms in my belly, and I nod.

He groans and pulls me flush against his body. My nipples rub against his chest, and the length of his cock is slick and warm between us.

"I can't fucking wait to watch you grow round and heavy with my baby," he says. "To know that the whole world will see what we've done."

His lips crash down hard on mine, and he kisses me like he can't get enough. He walks me backwards out of the spray of water and presses me up against the tile. I gasp, but his mouth doesn't leave mine. He's kissing me everywhere. My lips. My neck. My collarbone.

"Oh God," I moan.

Then he's turning me around, guiding my hands up onto the wet tiles to brace myself. "Keep your hands right there," he growls.

His hands slide around my front, and he cups my breasts, rolling my nipples between his fingers. My body arches against him, and he pushes a leg between my thighs, nudging them apart.

"Is this what you want, babygirl?" he whispers, his lips brushing my ear.

I can't even speak. I can barely breathe. All I can do is nod, and his hands slide lower. One goes down to tease my clit, while the other wraps around my thigh, lifting it. Opening me wider.

I moan as he starts to stroke the sensitive nub before dipping down to test how wet I am.

"You're already soaked," he groans.

I bite my lip. "Mmhmm."

He presses the blunt tip of his cock against my entrance, and I push back against him. He slips inside me, and he's not gentle like he was last night. He's hard and fast, and it's almost too much, but I love it.

"Yes," I pant. "Oh God, yes. Please."

"Fuck," he groans. "You're still so fucking tight, babygirl. Your little pussy was made for my cock."

He pounds into me, his thrusts so hard they send shockwaves through my body. His free hand tangles in my wet hair, pulling my head back against his chest, and I let out a moan.

"Is this how you want it, babygirl?" he grunts.

"Yes. Oh, God, yes. More. Please, give me more."

"I'm going to fuck a baby into you, sweetheart," he says, his voice rough and deep. "I'm going to make sure everyone knows you're mine."

His other hand moves back to my clit, circling it faster and faster, and all I can do is whimper and moan as his cock slams into me and his fingers stroke me. The pleasure is intense, almost painful, and my eyes squeeze shut.

"Come for me, babygirl," he says, and there's an edge of strain in his voice. Like he's barely hanging on. "I need to feel your pretty little cunt squeezing my cock."

My body is coiled tight, ready to spring, and with one more flick of his finger over my clit, I'm falling apart. I scream his name as my orgasm rushes through me, and then I feel the hot rush of his cum filling me. His hips jerk, his movements wild and unrestrained, and I know he's marking me. Claiming me. Making me his.

When he's spent, he slides out of me, but he doesn't let go. He holds me against his chest, his arms wrapped around me, and even though my legs are trembling and my whole body feels boneless, I've never felt more protected. More cared for.

"You're mine, Rosalie," he says, his lips at my ear. "Forever."

I close my eyes, and the words float through my mind like a wish.

Because, more than anything, I want this to be real.

Chapter Six

♥

Matteo

The sun's just barely up when I step onto the terrace, coffee in hand, the smell of salt in the air.

The house is still, like it's waiting for her to wake up. Like even the walls are learning to breathe with her in them.

I lean against the railing and watch the waves roll in. My fingers curl around the mug, but I'm not drinking. My mind's already running. It always does in the early hours, before she softens me with her pretty smile and her sleepy voice.

Two weeks. That's all it's been since I first touched her, claimed her, made her mine. And everything's different now. Every fucking thing.

I don't sleep much. Not because of nightmares or the kind of guilt most men like me carry. That's not my burden. I don't regret the things I've done. But lately, I stay awake because I don't want to miss a single moment of this. Of her.

I'm always listening for her footsteps before I even realize I'm doing it. That soft little padding sound she makes when she's still half-asleep and walking barefoot across the wood floors.

God, she's sweet. She used to move through the villa like someone who's only ever been expected to stay quiet. But in the past two weeks, she's been blooming. Slowly. Carefully. And fuck if it doesn't make something raw twist in my chest every time she laughs like she means it. Every time she reaches for me like I'm not a monster.

The door creaks open behind me and I turn towards the sound, already feeling my chest ease, like just seeing Rosalie is enough to anchor me.

She's barefoot and glowing. Hair messy, sleep still lingering in her eyes, and wearing one of my shirts so big it hits mid-thigh. She's holding something in her hand, fingers wrapped tight around it like she's afraid it might vanish. She stops and then smiles at me.

Beams, really.

I don't know what I expect her to say, but it sure as hell isn't what comes next.

"I'm pregnant."

The words hit like a punch to the chest. Not in a bad way. Never that. It's just... this is everything I've been wanting, planning, craving. And now it's real.

It takes half a second for me to move. I set my coffee on the railing and cross the space between us in two strides. She watches me with those wide eyes, her smile faltering just slightly like she doesn't know what I'll do.

So I drop to my knees right there on the terrace floor. I press my hands to her hips and lean in to kiss the soft curve of her stomach. There's nothing visible there yet. But I feel it. I feel everything when it comes to my babygirl.

I look up at her. "You're sure?"

She nods, tears welling in her eyes even as she smiles widely. "I took a test, and it's positive," she says, holding out the hand holding the test to show me.

A sharp exhale punches out of me as I bury my face against her belly again. She threads her fingers through my hair, and I swear I could stay like this forever.

But I can't. Not really. Because now that I know she's carrying my baby, my brain is already shifting into overdrive. Quietly calculating every threat. Every risk. Every possible move.

Because it's not just my woman I need to keep safe now. I have to protect our baby, too. And I'll burn the world down before I let anything touch either of them.

I rise to my feet and frame her face with my hands, brushing my thumbs over her cheeks. "We're leaving," I say.

Her brow furrows. "What? Why?"

"I want to take you somewhere safer, babygirl. My main estate is more secure. More of my people around who can help make sure no harm comes to you or the little one. I've got business to handle, and I don't want you left unguarded while I do it."

"Business?" she echoes.

I kiss her lips gently. "Nothing you need to worry about, babygirl. Just tying up loose ends."

What I don't say is that I've known who her father is for a while now. Knew who Gregory was the moment Luca sent me the email with all the details. Two spoiled little men with too much money and not enough soul. Men who think they are powerful and can do whatever they want, even trading Rosalie like a piece of property.

They'll learn soon enough there are men in the world far more dangerous than they could ever dream of being.

Rosalie looks up at me, a small smile tugging at the corner of her lips. "Does this mean I'll get to see more of your world?"

"You will," I promise.

She nods, glowing again. "Then I guess I should pack."

"You should. I love you, babygirl, and you've made me so damn happy today."

Her smile somehow brightens even more. "I love you too, Matteo." She rises onto tiptoes and presses a soft kiss to the corner of my lip, and that small touch sends a heat curling through my chest.

As she turns back into the house, humming to herself, I pull out my phone and text Luca.

We're coming home. Set up the meeting. It's time.

He replies within seconds.

Understood. I'll handle it.

I slip the phone away and look back out at the ocean, jaw tight, blood running hot beneath my skin. The time to play this defensively has passed. Now it's time to strike, to make sure those two men never get a chance to hurt my woman ever again.

This is what I was made for. This is who I am. Anyone who dares to threaten Rosalie or my baby will answer to me.

And they will pay in blood.

Chapter Seven

♥

Rosalie

The gates swing open, and my breath catches.

If I'd thought Matteo's villa had been impressive, it seems tiny compared to his main estate. Even the expensive home I'd grown up in pales in comparison. This place is massive. A long driveway curves through manicured lawns, lined with towering trees and flowers that look too perfect to be real. The building itself is stone and glass, sleek and solid, with sharp edges and high windows. It's beautiful, but in a powerful, intimidating kind of way.

"Home," Matteo says simply, one hand resting on my thigh as he drives.

It's hard to imagine ever feeling like I belong somewhere like this. But with him by my side, I already do.

He parks outside the front entrance. The front door opens before we've even gotten out of the car. A man stands waiting. Broad-shouldered, dark-haired, dressed all in black.

"This is Luca," Matteo says as we step out. "He's my right-hand man. The closest thing I've got to a brother. I trust him with everything."

Luca nods at me, the corners of his lips curling up into a hint of a smile. "It's a pleasure to finally meet you, Rosalie."

"Hi," I say, a little shyly. There's something calm about him, though, that helps me feel at ease almost instantly. Like he's seen a lot and doesn't scare easily. In that way, he reminds me of Matteo.

"He's the only man I trust to protect what's mine," Matteo adds as he wraps one arm around my waist and places his hand on my tummy.

My cheeks warm, but I don't look away. I like the way he says that, like it's a fact carved in stone.

Inside, the estate is even more impressive. The ceilings are high, the floors polished, the furniture expensive without being too flashy. There's art on the walls, subtle security cameras tucked into corners, the faint scent of leather and wood polish in the air.

It should feel cold. But somehow, it doesn't.

Matteo gives me a quick tour of the main living areas, and as we walk through the halls, I spot several men. All of them are big and armed. They all look curiously my way, but none of them approach or say anything.

I can see what Matteo means about this place having more security now.

When we reach the master suite, he wraps his arms around me from behind, resting his chin on my shoulder.

"I need to leave for my meeting now, babygirl. It can't be avoided, but I will come back to you as quickly as I can."

I turn to face him, circling my arms around his waist and resting my head against the solid muscle of his chest. "Are you going to be safe?"

He nods. "I'm taking a couple of my men with me. I'll be perfectly safe. And Luca will be here to take care of you, and there is other security around. Nobody will be able to get close to you."

I nod, but I'm still nervous. It's only been two weeks, but the thought that something might happen to him, that he might not come back to me, fills me with dread. Especially now that I'm carrying his baby inside me.

Matteo sees it in my face. He cups my cheek with one hand and leans in, brushing his lips over mine.

"I'll be back soon, Rosalie," he murmurs. "I promise."

He kisses me once more, longer this time, and then he's gone. Luca steps into the hallway nearby, his posture relaxed but alert.

"I'll wait out here until he gets back," he says. "If you need anything, just ask."

I give him a grateful smile, then step back into the bedroom, closing the door behind me.

***

It's been almost two hours.

I sit, then stand. Pace the length of the bedroom. Sit again.

The silence in this place is different from the quiet of Matteo's villa. There, the hush was peaceful. Here, it feels heavy. Like something bad is about to happen.

I glance at my phone for the hundredth time. Still nothing. No messages. No missed calls. He told me not to worry. He said it was just business. That he'd be back soon.

But soon is starting to feel like forever.

I stand at the window, staring out over the grounds. The sky has darkened slightly, the sun slipping lower, casting long shadows across the driveway.

I chew my bottom lip, consider texting him. Just a quick message to check in. But I stop myself. The last thing I want is to be the kind of partner who needs constant reassurance, who distracts him when he's doing something important.

But still... it's hard to fight the urge to contact him.

I turn from the window and start pacing again, arms wrapped around my middle. My stomach flips, and not in the good way.

A soft knock breaks the quiet.

I freeze. "Yes?"

The door creaks open. It's Luca. His face is unreadable, but he seems calm enough. "Rosalie." He steps into the room. "Matteo called. He got word of a threat that might be heading this way."

I go cold. "What kind of threat?"

"He didn't give me all the details. Only that we can't risk staying here any longer. He wants you moved to a secondary safe house immediately. He'll meet us there as soon as the meeting wraps up."

I blink at him. "Why didn't he call me?"

Luca's expression doesn't falter. "He didn't want to worry you. Said to move quickly and quietly. We need to leave. Now."

"Okay." I move on autopilot, every part of me feeling numb. The only good news from all this is that Matteo called Luca, so he must still be safe. I scoop up a jacket, and try to ignore the tight knot forming in my chest.

It's just a precaution. That's all. And Matteo will be waiting for me on the other end of this.

Luca leads me out of the bedroom and down the long hallway of the estate. Everything feels still, too quiet. It's probably just in my head, but I can't shake the nervous flutter in my stomach.

He holds the front door open for me and I step outside. One of Matteo's men, stationed near the gate, glances our way and approaches.

"Everything okay?" the man asks, his hand resting casually near the weapon holstered at his side.

Luca gives him a short nod. "Matteo asked me to relocate her to a secondary site. He's on his way there already to meet us."

The man's eyes flick to me, then back to Luca. "Copy that," he says after a beat. "Keep your phone on."

"Will do," Luca replies, already walking me towards the sleek black car waiting just beyond the gates.

As I slide into the passenger seat, my thoughts drift straight to Matteo. He promised he'd be fine. But the idea of some threat being out there, something dangerous enough to move me without warning, makes my chest tighten.

I don't ask any questions. I just buckle my seatbelt and press my hands into my lap, forcing myself to stay calm while Luca switches on the engine and pulls away.

Please be okay, Matteo. Please come back to me.

The roads are unfamiliar, winding through industrial stretches I don't recognize. Not residential. Not scenic. Just gray buildings and empty lots. Luca keeps his eyes on the road, his jaw locked tight.

I glance over at him, trying to keep my voice casual. "So... where exactly are we going?"

"A safe location," he says, clipped.

"Right, but where?" I press. "What kind of place?"

He doesn't answer.

My fingers tangle together nervously in my lap. "Luca?"

"Matteo gave instructions," he says, still not looking at me. "I'm just following them."

A cold little pinprick of doubt creeps down my spine. Something doesn't feel right.

I glance out the window again. There's nothing around us now. No signs, no other cars. Just a wide, cracked stretch of asphalt ahead, and a building in the distance. An abandoned building, by the looks of it.

Luca pulls the car to a slow stop in front of the warehouse. The engine cuts. He still won't look at me.

My heart starts to pound. "Why are we stopping here?"

Finally, he turns his head. And what I see in his eyes makes my blood go cold.

Guilt. Real, raw guilt.

"I'm sorry," he says, voice low. "I didn't have a choice."

I stare at him. "What are you talking about?"

He opens his mouth, but nothing comes out.

I don't wait for more. I fumble with the door and step out of the car, my legs shaking slightly as I plant my feet on the gravel. The air feels thick. Like it's holding its breath.

Then the warehouse doors creak open, and Gregory steps out. The man I ran from on our wedding day.

He's calm. Smirking at me like he's pretty damn proud of himself. And the sight of him hits me like a punch to the chest. I can't move. Can't breathe.

His smirk turns into a wide smile. "Hello, darling," he says. "Did you miss me?"

Chapter Eight

♥

Matteo

The elevator dings softly as it opens onto the top floor of the building I own. Glass and steel stretch out before me, and it's the kind of luxury that intimidates men who don't belong in it. Good. That's the point.

I step out, suit sharp, shirt black, no tie. I don't desire to feel as if I have a noose around my neck. My men fall into place beside me. Nico and Lorenzo. They are my silent shadows with loaded weapons, and I've given them orders to shoot if our guests so much as blink wrong. The air is chilled. Still. Waiting.

I expect two men in that room up ahead. Two men who mistreated my woman, and who will not get another opportunity to repeat that mistake.

My jaw clenches as I walk the corridor, the hush of polished floors beneath our shoes the only sound.

I push open the door to the meeting room, pausing for a moment when I see only one man is sitting at the table.

Her father, Victor. Where the fuck is Gregory?

Victor rises to his feet too quickly, trying to look calm, but his hands betray him as they twitch nervously at his sides. I can smell fear. The air is thick with it in here. And I know it's not because of guilt. I doubt a weasel like him is capable of feeling that emotion. It's because he knows what will happen to him if he doesn't agree to my demands.

"Matteo," he says, like we're old friends. Like I don't want to drag him across this floor and make him regret every word he ever said to his daughter.

"You're alone," I say flatly.

He nods once. "Gregory couldn't make it."

Convenient.

I take two slow steps closer, lowering my voice to that tone that never fails to terrify my enemies. "Listen carefully, Victor. I don't want there to be any confusion. I will not be letting you or Gregory anywhere near Rosalie. And if you or that arrogant little prick you promised her to ever so much as look in her direction again, it will be the last thing either of you do."

Victor holds up both hands, palms out. "Matteo, I hear you. I have no interest in fighting. Truly. If she's happy with you, then I'm not going to try and take her away from you. I'm not the monster of a father you believe me to be. All I want is for my daughter to be happy."

I narrow my eyes as I listen to him. My bullshit detectors are pinging off the fucking charts, and I don't buy a word of it. For a man who had been desperate enough to sell her off for a fortune only a few weeks ago, he seems awfully calm about losing his biggest bargaining chip.

He's hiding something. I can practically taste it on him. And I don't like it. This man might be my future father-in-law, but I will not allow anything to threaten the safety and happiness of my new family.

Without taking my eyes off him, I address my men.

"Nico. Lorenzo. You are going to stay here with Victor and do whatever you have to do to get information out of him. He's planning something, and I want to know what it is."

Victor's eyes widen, and his mouth opens like he's going to protest, but I'm already walking out of the room while Lorenzo and Nico close in on him.

"Let me know as soon as you find out what he's up to, gentlemen," I say as I walk out of the office.

I've been away from Rosalie too long already, and if Victor is plotting something, then I want to get back to her sooner rather than later.

***

By the time I get back to my estate, there is a heavy feeling in the pit of my stomach. I just need to see Rosalie. I need to hold her. One second with her in my arms and this ugly feeling might settle.

I barely let the engine cool before I'm out of the car, taking long strides towards the front doors. Every step sharp, purposeful. My mind's been churning since I left Victor. Something about his surrender didn't sit right.

I walk straight to the bedroom, knowing it's where I left her, and I'd be surprised if she felt comfortable enough to explore the place without me.

It's empty. Fuck.

"Rosalie?" My voice cuts through the air like a blade. There's no answer.

I check the ensuite. Nothing. The balcony. No trace. I move faster now, searching other rooms. The kitchen. Library. One of the sitting rooms. Every single one is empty.

I head back to the bedroom, reaching for my phone and dialing her number. Just as I do, I notice hers sitting on the nightstand. The screen lights up with my name. She's not going to answer because she doesn't even have the damn thing with her.

I try to push down the fear rising up inside me. I need to keep my head clear. I can't let myself succumb to those other feelings until I know she's safe. Until I know my woman and our baby are unharmed.

I call Luca.

The phone rings, but no one answers.

"Fuck!" My curse echoes off the walls.

I need to stay calm. Rational. Luca is smart. He's loyal. There's no way he would let anyone harm a hair on her head.

But the fact remains that they're not here. And Gregory was not at the meeting.

I'm halfway down the hallway when one of my men rounds the corner. His eyes grow wide when he sees me.

"Boss, what are you doing here? Luca told me you were going to meet them at a different safe house."

I stop dead in my tracks.

"What the fuck did you just say?" My voice is low. Deadly.

The guys blinks, clearly realizing he's just stepped into something dangerous. "Luca said you'd contacted him. Said there was a threat, and you wanted Rosalie moved to a secondary location. I thought..."

"You thought?" I take a step closer as I cut him off, and my ice cold tone makes him visibly flinch. "You didn't check with me? You didn't confirm the order came from me? You just let him fucking take her?"

He's starting to sweat. "I'm sorry, Boss. It was Luca. I trusted him."

So did I. And now they're gone.

My vision goes red.

I'm on him before he can move, hand wrapping around his throat as I slam him into the wall. His eyes bulge, face turning purple. He claws at my arm, trying to break free, but my grip doesn't relent.

I've snapped. Broken. Gone wild.

I squeeze harder. His mouth opens, desperate to suck in a breath.

I could kill him. The bastard deserves it for letting Rosalie leave. I should've known better than to trust anyone but myself.

The last bit of air leaves his lungs, and his eyes roll back.

My teeth clench. I need to think. Need to breathe. Need to figure out where the hell my woman has gone.

With a frustrated growl, I release my grip. The man drops to the ground, coughing, gasping.

"Get eyes on everything. Start with the estate's surveillance. Every camera. Every angle. I want footage of Luca leaving with her. Time-stamp it. Track the car from the second it pulled out."

He nods vigorously, his fingers gently touching the red marks that are already appearing on his neck.

"Then pull traffic cam footage from every street within a ten-mile radius. Work outwards. I want local businesses, gas stations, parking lots. Anything with a feed. Find his car. Find the route. And get a drone in the air if we need one."

"Yes, Boss," he says, scrambling to his feet.

I snarl the last order before he can take a step. "I want her location in the next fifteen minutes, or I swear to God someone's going to lose their fucking head for this."

The guard bolts like his life depends on it. Which, to be fair, it might.

I storm into my office, slamming the door behind me so hard that the walls shudder.

They took her. They fucking took her from me.

And now there will be nowhere on this earth safe enough to hide them from what's coming.

Chapter Nine

♥

Rosalie

The warehouse is colder than I expected. Damp, too. It's the kind of cold that sinks into your bones, no matter how tightly you wrap your arms around yourself.

Luca's hand is firm on my arm as he pushes me forward. I stumble slightly as I try to drag my feet, trying to delay the moment where I will be standing right in front of the man I left at the altar.

Gregory is just standing there with his arms folded, wearing that smug little grin that I hate. The one that used to make my skin crawl every time he directed it at me.

"Well done," he says to Luca, almost like he's praising a toddler for eating their broccoli. "You're right on time."

Luca nods, not really looking at either of us. I glare at him, hoping he will feel it. It's the least he deserves for betraying me and Matteo.

"Tell me something, Luca," Gregory continues. "If you've known where she was this whole time, why didn't you let us handle it sooner? Why wait? You could have told us where they've been hiding and we could have grabbed her ourselves."

Luca hesitates just for a second. Then he speaks, low and tired. "Because if you'd tried to grab her while Matteo was around, he would've killed every last one of us before we made it ten feet. You think I want to die over your ego?"

My heart twists, but I don't let it show. Luca was planning this the whole time. The man who is apparently like a brother to Matteo. The only one Matteo felt could be trusted with me and his baby.

My heart shatters for the man I love, but I don't break. I can't. I won't.

I let my arms drop to my stomach, pressing my hands over the small curve that isn't even showing yet while sending a silent promise to the little life growing inside me that I won't ever let anything hurt it.

Gregory's fingers close around my arm. He's not rough, but his hold on me is firm enough to make it clear I don't have a say in what happens next. That doesn't stop me from considering whether or not I can get away. If I can run. But at the moment, it's two much bigger, stronger men, against one woman. I don't stand a chance. So, for now, I comply.

He drags me through a maze of corridors, past several armed men, into a smaller room. It's darker in here. No windows. The only light comes from a flickering bulb above us that buzzes like it's struggling to stay alive. The walls are bare concrete, the floor cracked and stained.

There's a single chair waiting at the far end of the room with rope lying on the floor beside it. He pushes me into the chair and starts tying my wrists to the armrests before moving to secure my ankles to the thick wooden legs.

My heart is beating so fast I can feel it in my throat, but I force my breathing to stay even. No struggling. No screaming. I need to make sure I don't do anything that will cause him hurt me or the baby before Matteo arrives. And I know he will come for us.

He steps back, tilting his head as he looks me over. Then he starts paces the small room, slow and steady. He examines me with his eyes like a predator deciding where to sink its teeth.

"You made me look like a fool, Rosalie," he says. "Do you have any idea how that felt?"

I keep my eyes forward.

"You humiliated me," he snaps, voice rising. "Everyone saw it. The way you ran away from me like I was nothing."

I say nothing. I wouldn't know what to say, anyway. The man is crazy.

"After everything I did for you," he growls. "I gave you everything. And you spit in my face by finding some other guy almost instantly. You think he's going to love you the way I did? He probably just sees you as a temporary little fucktoy. When he gets bored of you, or when he knocks you up, he'll throw you away like the piece of trash you are."

I close my eyes for a second. Just one. Just long enough to picture Matteo. The way his arms feel around me, the low rumble of his voice when he tells me everything's going to be okay. The fire in his eyes when he looks at me like I'm his whole world.

I hold on to that. I hold on to him. And I don't say a word.

He leans down close to my face. I flinch before I can stop myself. His fingers trail along my shoulder and I feel every muscle in my body go tight.

"You're going to marry me," he says firmly, like only he gets to decide my future. "You don't get to run away from me. I paid for you, and you're mine."

I open my eyes to meet his.

"You can't buy a person, Gregory," I say quietly. "And you definitely can't own me."

He stares at me like he doesn't understand the words. Like logic is a foreign language he's too arrogant to learn.

"I don't love you. I never did. And no matter what you do, no matter how long you keep me here, I never will."

The tension snaps. He explodes.

"You think this is about love?" he roars, slamming his palm into the wall right beside my head. The sound cracks through the room like a gunshot.

I flinch, but I don't look away. His breath is ragged. His face blotched red with fury.

"You think that bastard loves you? He's not coming for you. You're nothing to him. He'll cut his losses and find another whore before the day's out."

I don't answer. I won't feed his delusion.

Gregory scoffs and steps back, pacing a few feet like he needs to burn off whatever twisted emotion is pulsing through him.

"I gave you a chance to make this easy," he mutters. "But fine. We'll do it the hard way."

He heads toward the door.

"Gregory..." I say, but he doesn't turn around.

He steps out and slams it behind him. The lock clicks and silence falls as I'm left alone in the small room.

I lean my head back against the wall behind me and close my eyes, letting the same thought run through my mind over and over.

Hold on, little one. Daddy's coming for us.

Chapter Ten

♥

Matteo

The night is as thick as oil.

No moon. No stars. Just fog crawling low along the ground and the steady hum of engines as our convoy pulls in. A row of matte-black SUVs glides to a stop in front of the warehouse like a pack of wolves closing in for the kill. One by one, doors open. My men spill out. Silent. Armed. Lethal. They move like they've done this a hundred times. Because they have.

I wait until the last door opens before stepping out.

The air is cold enough to bite. My breath fogs as I cross the gravel, each step slow, deliberate. I'm dressed in black from head to toe. Wool coat, gloves, the weight of my weapon a steady pressure at my side. Every inch of me is controlled, calculated.

I'm going to find her. And I'm going to end anyone who stands in my way.

My men fall into formation without a word, waiting for orders. I don't raise my voice. I don't need to.

"Gregory dies on sight," I say, voice low but razor sharp. "No hesitation. No warnings. You see him, you put him down."

There's a murmur of confirmation. No one questions me. They wouldn't dare.

"Luca is mine, though," I add, my voice cold. Deadly. "If you find him, keep hold of him until I'm ready to deal with him."

I turn to the two men standing closest to me. "Two of my men are already with Victor," I tell them. "I want you two to join them."

They nod, already turning toward the car, but I'm not done.

"Tell him he has twelve hours to get out of the country. If I so much as hear his name after that, he's a dead man." I pause before giving them my next instruction. "Make sure he understands. Make it hurt just enough that he won't even consider trying to come back for his daughter."

They disappear back into the SUV. Doors slam. Tires crunch gravel. The car spins out onto the dark road, taillights disappearing into the fog.

I turn back toward the warehouse. It looms in front of us, all concrete and silence, crouched in the dark like it knows what's coming.

My eyes scan the exterior. Every corner. Every shadow. I can practically hear her breathing inside. I can feel the pull of her like gravity.

Rosalie.

I nod once, sharply.

It's time to bring her home.

The warehouse door gives under pressure with a low metallic groan. The instant it opens, we flood inside, shadows slipping through shadows.

No words. Just motion.

The first guard barely has time to register we're there before he drops. One shot, center mass. My men drag his body back into the dark without breaking stride. Another to the left has his throat slit clean. No noise. No hesitation.

We move like a machine. Clean. Cold. Purpose-built for this moment.

My gun is drawn, weight familiar in my hand. My pulse is steady. My mind is fire.

She's here. Somewhere in this concrete tomb. And I will find her.

We clear hallways like snapping wires. Room by room, corridor by corridor. Flashlights slice through the dark. Boots hit the floor in practiced rhythm. Another guard. Another body. They barely even slow us down.

"Visual on the target!" someone calls through the comms.

A shot rings out. Followed by a single, sickening thud.

I pivot just in time to catch a glimpse of Gregory's body sprawled on his back in a widening pool of blood. One of my men lowers his weapon without a flicker of emotion.

That's it. That's him.

Dead.

There's a flash of satisfaction. Something sharp and cold, buried under layers of rage and need. But I don't linger on it. I don't need to. He's not important anymore.

He's not the point.

She is.

I press forward, faster now. Every second that ticks by is another I don't have her in my arms. Another breath I can't take until I see her face.

The hallway narrows ahead. There's one final door.

One of my men steps aside the moment I reach it, face pale, nodding once.

"She must be in there," he says, voice low.

I don't wait.

My boot hits the door with enough force to crack the frame, and I'm inside before it finishes swinging open.

And there she is. Tied to a chair. Hair tangled. Wrists red. Her face pale but her eyes...

Her eyes find mine. Wide. Shining. Alive.

My heart stops. For a second, everything in me just stops.

Then I'm moving.

Two steps. Maybe three. I'm on my knees in front of her, already working at the ropes. My hands shake, but I keep them steady. I have to. She needs calm. She needs me.

"It's over," I murmur, voice low. Fierce. "I've got you."

The ropes fall away and she doesn't hesitate. Rosalie crashes into me like a wave, arms around my neck, face pressed to my chest.

I catch her. Hold her. Wrap myself around her like a fortress. I bury my face in her hair and breathe her in like oxygen.

She's here. She's whole. She's mine.

My hand finds her belly before I even think about it. My throat tightens. My chest aches.

They're both safe.

I kiss her hair. Her forehead. Her hands.

"I'm here," I whisper, over and over. "You're safe now. I've got you."

She tilts her head up to look at me, and even through the exhaustion and fear, there's something unshakable in her eyes.

"I knew you'd come for me," she whispers. "I never doubted it. Not for a second."

I pause. Press my lips to her temple.

"You're mine," I say simply. "I'll always come for you."

We make it halfway down the corridor when two of my men round the corner, dragging a figure between them.

Luca.

He's cuffed. Pale. Shaking.

They throw him to the ground like garbage, and he lands hard on his knees, arms behind his back. Rosalie flinches beside me. I pull her slightly behind me and step forward, slow and deliberate.

Gun still in hand. Not raised. Not yet.

Luca won't meet my eyes. He's trembling so badly he looks like he might fall over.

"Why?" I ask. One word. Low. Razor sharp.

That's all it takes. Luca breaks like glass.

"I was drowning," he gasps. "I didn't mean for it to get this far. I... God, Matteo, I was stupid. I owed money. A lot of it. To the wrong people. They were circling. I thought they were going to kill me."

His voice cracks. He won't stop talking now.

"Gregory came to me. Offered me a way out. Money. Protection. Said no one would get hurt. He said you wouldn't risk starting a war over a woman."

My jaw clenches so tight I taste blood.

He looks up then, and the tears are real, but I feel nothing for them.

"You should have come to me," I say, my voice so cold he flinches.

"I was ashamed," he whispers. "I couldn't face you. Not like this. You were always... better. Stronger. I knew what you'd think of me."

My voice is quiet when I answer. Dead quiet.

"You were like a brother to me. All you had to do was come to me. I would have helped you. Taken care of it all. But instead..."

I pause. Let the words land with all the condemnation they deserve.

"... you handed my woman, and my baby, to the enemy."

I don't speak again right away. I just stare down at him, the man I thought of as my brother, as he kneels in the dust and broken silence, shaking, pale, undone.

The air in the room feels frozen, stretched tight across the space like it might snap. No one moves. No one dares to breathe.

Luca doesn't beg. He knows what is about to happen.

I let the silence grow, let it wrap around us like a noose. Let the weight of his betrayal hang in the air between us.

Then, finally, I speak quietly. "Any last words?"

His throat bobs as he swallows. His eyes flick up, just for a second. There's no fight in them. No hope. Just a flicker of understanding. Of acceptance.

He shakes his head.

I raise the gun. Pull the trigger.

One clean shot. No hesitation. No drama. Just the sound of an ending.

I turn away before the body hits the ground, and walk back to the only thing that still matters in this world.

Rosalie steps into my arms, her face against my chest. I press a kiss to the top of her head, letting the feel of her ground me. Steady me. Bring me back to life.

I cup her chin and tilt her face up so I can look at her. Really look at her. She's safe. She's here. She's mine.

"Let's go home," I murmur.

She nods, fingers tangling in mine, her grip like a lifeline.

We walk together, out into the night, knowing that she is safe now and that I will do what I can to always keep her that way.

Chapter Eleven

♥

Rosalie

Matteo's hand never leaves the small of my back as he leads me across the gravel. His steps are slow and steady, almost like he's afraid I'll break if he moves too fast. Maybe I will. I'm not sure yet.

The car waiting for us is black and sleek, its surface gleaming under the moonlight like obsidian. The door's already open. He helps me in with the kind of care that makes my throat tighten. Like I'm something precious.

I glance back. Just once. The warehouse stands silent in the dark, windows blown out, shadows moving through the wreckage. Matteo's men are everywhere. I can't see their faces, but I don't need to. I know what they're doing. What they're cleaning up.

The sight makes my stomach twist, and I force myself to turn away.

"You've seen enough," Matteo says quietly, as he gets in beside me. His voice is steady, but there's something in it. Something hard. "I'm getting you out of here."

I nod. I don't say anything. I don't need to.

He starts the engine, and we roll forward into the night. Away from the chaos. Away from the blood.

My fingers find his without thinking. I clutch his hand like it's the only thing anchoring me to the earth. And maybe it is.

The silence in the car stretches out around us. It's not uncomfortable. Just... full. My body's still humming with fear, with adrenaline, with exhaustion I can feel all the way down to my bones.

And yet I can't stop thinking about the way he looked just before he pulled the trigger on Luca.

Cold. Controlled. Unflinching.

Some part of me should be afraid of that, maybe. But I'm not. Not even a little. Because I know who that coldness was for.

And I know who the warmth is saved for.

Me. I know without a doubt that the man beside me would never hurt me. It's a truth I feel down to my very soul.

The road stretches ahead, quiet and endless. The headlights slice through the dark, casting long shadows that flicker and vanish as we pass. I rest my head back against the seat, still holding Matteo's hand like it's the only real thing in the world.

His phone buzzes in the center console.

He answers with a low, clipped, "Yeah."

Silence follows as he listens, his eyes never leaving the road. A few short nods. One-word replies.

"Good."

"Understood."

He ends the call and sets the phone back down, his fingers tightening around mine before he even speaks.

"Victor's gone," he says simply. "My men watched him board the plane."

I don't say anything. I just... let it sit.

Gone.

The word floats around inside me, bumping into things. Memories of him. Anger. A hundred unanswered questions.

My father is gone. And I don't know what I'm supposed to feel.

There's a part of me, small and buried, that thinks I should cry. That I should ache for the father who raised me. The one who tucked me in when I was little, who kissed my forehead and told me everything would be okay.

But that version of him disappeared a long time ago.

The man who sold me wasn't a father. Not really. The man who distracted Matteo while I was kidnapped… he made his choice.

Maybe one day I'll cry for him. Maybe I'll wake up and feel the loss like a hole in my chest. But not tonight.

Tonight, I'm just glad he's gone.

"Thank you," I whisper, not even sure what part I'm thanking Matteo for. All of it, maybe.

"You never have to thank me, babygirl," he murmurs. "Not for protecting what's mine."

I squeeze his fingers a little tighter. The fear, the horror, the rough ropes on my wrists… they're all fading now, replaced by something else. Something hotter. Something I can't hold back anymore.

It's him.

The way he holds the steering wheel in one hand, the other still tangled with mine. The quiet power in every line of his body. The way he looked at me in that warehouse, like he would tear the world apart for me.

He did. And now I need him.

Not just close. I need him on me, around me, inside me. I need to feel him erase every trace of what just happened with his hands, his mouth, his love.

I lean across the console slowly, letting my lips find his jaw. I press a kiss there. And another.

"But I should thank you," I whisper against his neck before placing a kiss there. "You saved me, Matteo."

My hand trails down his chest and rests high on his thigh, where the fabric of his pants does nothing to hide the way his body responds to my touch.

"Rosalie," he warns, voice rough, low, like gravel dragging over silk.

But I don't stop. My fingertips move higher, tracing the outline of his cock through his pants. I feel him throb, as if his hard flesh is seeking more.

Matteo growls, really growls, and it lights something deep in my belly.

"Keep touching me like that," he says, "and I'll pull over right now to show you all the ways you belong to me."

My pulse skips. I look up at him, my voice barely a whisper. "That's what I need, Matteo."

The tires crunch sharply as he jerks the wheel, turning off the road without a word.

Trees rise on either side, thick and shadowed, keeping us hidden from the main road.

He kills the engine, and I know what's coming.

And my entire body is tingling with anticipation.

Matteo climbs out of the car and rushes around to my side, opening my door and taking my hand to pull me out towards him. Then I'm in his arms, and for a moment, we just stand there.

His hands grip my waist. My fingers twist in the fabric of his shirt. Our breathing is uneven. Shaky. Full of so many unspoken promises.

Then he kisses me.

Hard. Desperate. Like he needs me more than oxygen. Like if he doesn't feel my mouth on his, he'll fall apart right here in the dirt.

His hands find my hair. My back. My ass. He pulls me flush against him, and the heat of his body makes me dizzy. The need is a roar in my ears, a wildfire spreading through me, consuming everything.

He walks me backward until I bump into the hood of the car. His hands slide down, and before I can think, he's lifted me onto it. His knee pushes between my thighs, spreading them, making me gasp.

His cock strains against the fabric of his pants. Hard. Throbbing.

My mouth goes dry.

Matteo grips the hem of my dress and shoves it roughly up my legs. He looks down at the bare skin of my thighs and my lace panties, and when his eyes flash, there's no more control left in them.

There's just a man possessed.

His fingers hook in the elastic waistband, and he rips them clean off my body. The tearing sound is like gasoline on the flames. I gasp. My head falls back.

His hand slides up my thigh.

"Look at me, babygirl," he rasps.

My eyes find his, and the desire in them makes my whole body burn.

"You're mine," he murmurs, thumb stroking my inner thigh. "Tell me you're mine."

"Yours," I breathe.

"I won't stop until I hear you scream," he says, low and deadly.

"Oh god," I moan.

Then his hand is between my legs, his fingers teasing my wet slit, and all I can do is whimper.

He doesn't waste any time. He knows what I need.

Two fingers push inside me, stretching me, making me cry out. His thumb finds my clit and presses, light, rhythmic, merciless.

My nails dig into his shoulder. My thighs shake. I'm so wet it's almost embarrassing, but the way he looks at me, like I'm his salvation, his undoing, his everything... it just makes the heat grow.

His mouth finds mine. Our tongues collide. I taste his lips. His tongue.

He swallows the desperate little sounds I make as he curls his fingers inside me. As his thumb makes circles on my clit, faster, harder, sending shocks of pleasure through my body.

"Don't stop," I gasp. "Please don't stop. I'm so close."

"I don't plan to stop until your legs are too weak to carry you, Rosalie. You'll be feeling me for days, and that's a promise."

He crouches between my legs, his fingers still buried deep inside me, and presses his mouth to my thigh.

I can feel the heat of his breath on my skin, and it sends shivers up my spine.

"Mine," he murmurs, lips on my thigh.

"Yours," I echo.

His teeth graze my skin. Nibble. Suckle. "All mine."

Then his mouth is on my clit, and he's sucking, his tongue swirling over the sensitive bundle of nerves, and all I can do is whimper and buck and hold on to his hair like a lifeline.

He's ruthless. Hungry. His fingers curl inside me as his tongue drives me toward the edge.

I'm falling. Tumbling. Losing control.

He doesn't stop. Doesn't let up.

I'm gasping. Moaning. Trembling.

My back arches. My hips grind against his face.

Then the wave breaks.

Pleasure rips through me, fast and furious, stealing my breath, my thoughts, my words. It's all I can do to cling to him as my body shakes, as my muscles tense, as my toes curl.

It goes on and on.

My head falls back. My eyes flutter closed.

He works me through it, his touch relentless, his mouth hot and hungry, until finally, the waves start to ebb.

When I finally come back to myself, he's kissing the inside of my thigh again.

"Fuck," he whispers, so softly I almost miss it.

I look down at him. Find his eyes. They're dark. Fierce. Full of hunger and need.

My pulse quickens.

"I'm not done with you yet, babygirl," he says, voice low.

Without another word, he rises. His mouth is on me again, except this time, his lips are brushing against my stomach, his hands caressing the soft flesh there as if he can feel the life growing inside.

Then his hands are moving again, gathering the fabric of my dress, sliding it slowly up. Too eager to wait, I grab the hem and pull it off over my head, leaving me bare save for my bra.

The cold air makes my skin prickle, and my nipples harden against the lace.

Matteo doesn't hesitate. His mouth finds my breasts. His tongue teases the hard peaks through the fabric.

I gasp, fingers tangling in his hair.

My legs are still trembling, but the need is already building again, low and heavy and undeniable.

His lips move over my body, and his hands roam. He doesn't rush. He takes his time. Like he's savoring every inch of me.

When his mouth reaches my breasts again, he tugs the lace cups down, and his tongue finds the bare skin. My nipple. The underside of my breast. Everywhere.

I'm lost in the sensation. Lost in him.

My hands fumble with his shirt buttons, and he straightens, shrugging out of it as his eyes find mine.

"I want you inside me," I say, voice shaking, fingers moving to the buttons of his pants.

His hand covers mine. "I will be."

He unbuttons the fly and frees his cock. The sight of it is enough to make my mouth water.

I reach for him, desperate, eager, but he pushes my hand away before gripping the base of his shaft and guiding the blunt head to my entrance.

He drags it over the slickness there. Teases me. Tortures me. I can't breathe. I can't speak. All I can do is beg with my body. With the way I'm arching towards him. The way my legs part for him. The way my nails dig into his arm.

I need him. I need him now.

And when he finally pushes inside me, inch by slow, perfect inch, I gasp.

He fills me. Stretches me. Completes me.

"Oh god," I moan.

His body presses against mine, skin on skin, and he feels like heaven.

"You're mine," he says against the shell of my ear.

"Yes."

"I'll never let anyone hurt you. Not ever again. Even if it means never letting you out of my sight for the rest of my life." His hand slides down, rests against my stomach, his touch reverent. "I will do whatever it takes to protect you both."

"Matteo," I gasp.

The intensity in his eyes. The way his hand cradles my stomach. It's too much.

He pulls back. Then he's pushing inside me again, a little harder this time, a little deeper. My eyes flutter closed, and the sensation washes over me like warm waves on the sand.

"Look at me, babygirl," he grunts, as he picks up the pace.

My eyes fly open, and the hunger I see in his is enough to make my knees weak.

He pounds into me, rough, relentless, and I take him. All of him.

Every muscle in his body is coiled tight. Tense. His jaw is clenched. His eyes never leave mine.

"Harder," I gasp.

He growls and drives into me. Again. Again. Again. The sound of flesh on flesh is almost obscene, but it only fuels the fire.

"God, Matteo. Yes. Fuck. Please."

My nails rake down his back, and he doesn't even flinch. He just fucks me harder.

His hands are on my hips, gripping so hard I know I'll have bruises, but I don't care. I want the bruises. I want the marks. I want him to claim me so deeply that no one will ever doubt who I belong to.

The orgasm builds inside me, slow at first, then growing like a storm.

Matteo's movements are getting frantic, his thrusts shallow, his grip tighter. I can feel his cock twitching, swelling, and I know he's close.

"Come for me, babygirl," he grunts. "I don't know if I can hold on much longer."

His words send a shiver through me, and then I'm lost. My body tenses. My back arches. The world explodes.

The orgasm rips through me, hard and fast and brutal. It's like falling. Like drowning. Like dying.

"Oh god. Oh god. Oh god," I moan.

Every inch of my skin is hot. My toes curl. My legs shake. Pleasure surges through me, wave after wave, until all I can do is gasp his name.

He groans, and his grip tightens. His cock throbs. Then he's coming too, spilling inside me, filling me, marking me, claiming me.

When it's over, we collapse in a heap on the hood of the car, bodies tangled, breaths coming in sharp gasps.

"Fuck, Rosalie," he whispers. "I don't know what I'd do if anything happened to you."

"You saved me," I whisper back. "You saved us."

"Always," he murmurs. "Forever."

We stay like that for a long time, wrapped in each other's arms, our breathing slowing, our hearts settling.

I breathe him in. Every part of me feels calmer now. Softer. Like the ache inside me has finally found a place to rest.

He presses a kiss to my temple, slow and lingering. Then he whispers, "Time to take you home, babygirl."

Home. I feel the word sink into my chest, and for a second, I hesitate.

I tilt my face up to his. "Is it wrong that when you say home... I think of the villa? Not the estate?"

His eyes find mine, and something in them softens. Then he smiles.

"Then I'll take you back to the villa. First thing in the morning." His knuckles brush my cheek. "We'll stay as long as you want. Forever, if that's what makes you happy."

His response makes my throat tighten and my heart swell. I nod against his chest. Let myself melt into his arms.

And as he helps me back into the car, as we drive off into the sleeping night, I close my eyes and listen to the soft little whisper in my head.

This is it. This is where everything begins.

Epilogue

♥

Matteo

Six months later:

The air smells like rosemary and wildflowers. Sunlight spills in golden stripes across the villa's garden, and for once in my life, everything is quiet.

No deals. No enemies. No shadows waiting at the edge of peace.

Just Rosalie.

I stand at the end of a narrow aisle cut through the grass, my heart beating a little faster than I'd like to admit. There are only a handful of people here. Just the ones who matter. My men who stood by me after Luca's betrayal, all of them cleaned up for once. A few of her friends I barely know but have already sworn to protect.

I don't even hear the music when it starts. Just the sound of my own breath, and then the soft rustle of fabric as the guests turn.

Then I see her. And I forget how to breathe.

Rosalie steps into the sunlight like a dream spun out of something softer than this world. Barefoot. Glowing. A wreath of tiny white flowers woven through her hair. No veil, just waves of chestnut silk spilling over her shoulders.

And beneath the soft folds of her dress, her belly rounds out proudly, beautifully, the clearest proof of what we've built together.

She walks slowly, one hand resting on her stomach, the other holding a small bouquet from the garden that she picked herself.

When her eyes meet mine, my bride blushes. Sweet and radiant.

She's the most beautiful thing I've ever seen.

But the best part, the part that makes my heart clench in my chest, is the way she's looking at me. Like nothing else exists in the world except us.

I've spent my entire life waiting for this moment. I knew the first time I saw her that she was supposed to be mine. To be the woman I spent the rest of my life with. And now, seeing her walk towards me, it's a truth I feel down to my bones.

She walks straight to me, and when she gets close enough, I reach for her hand.

Her fingers slip into mine like they've always belonged there.

The officiant clears his throat softly, but it's like we're wrapped in a bubble no one else can touch. I barely hear the words being spoken. Not because they don't matter, but because I already know what's true.

Her vows come in a soft, trembling voice, and she has to pause once, her hand pressed protectively over her belly, like she's grounding herself in the life we've made. I see a tear slip down her cheek, and I swipe it away with my thumb before she even blinks.

When it's my turn, I take her other hand, both of us breathing a little harder than we were a moment ago.

"I've done a lot of things I'm not proud of," I begin, and she nods, brave and unflinching.

"But loving you is the best thing I've ever done. The only thing I've ever done right from the beginning. And I will spend every breath I have making sure you feel that. You and the child we created. You'll never know fear again. Not while I'm alive."

Her eyes are glassy now. But her smile... her smile could tear down kingdoms.

The officiant speaks again, but this time I hear it.

"You may kiss the bride."

And I do. I kiss her like she's the only prayer I've ever believed in.

Around us, there's soft applause. A few whistles. Someone sniffles into a tissue. But none of it reaches me.

It's just us, and the new life blooming between us, wrapped in sunlight and hope.

About the Author

♥

Welcome to my wild, wicked world of *over-the-top, heart-pounding instalove*. I write fast-paced, **spicy age gap novellas** that don't waste time. They are just pure heat, obsession, and unapologetic desire from page one. If you're into dominant older heroes, eager younger heroines, and deliciously deviant themes like **breeding** and **lactation**, you're in the right place.

These days, all my stories revolve around one irresistible idea: **men who fall fast, fall hard, and never let go**. Think possessive, primal, borderline unhinged alphas who'd burn the world down for their girl. They're obsessed, they're intense, and yes, more than one has been lovingly described as a full-blown *caveman* by reviewers.

So whether you're here for the age gaps, the obsession, or the kind of heat that leaves scorch marks, you're in the right place. Get comfortable. It's about to get *feral*.

Find Willow online at https://allmylinks.com/willow-watkins

Printed in Dunstable, United Kingdom